Dazzling Travis

A STORY ABOUT BEING CONFIDENT & ORIGINAL

BY HANNAH CARMONA

ILLUSTRATED BY BRENDA FIGUEROA

DAZZLING TRAVIS: A STORY ABOUT BEING CONFIDENT & ORIGINAL

Copyright 2019 by Hannah Carmona
All rights reserved. First Edition 2019.
Printed in China and published by
Cardinal Rule Press.

Summary: Travis stands up for himself, reminding us to never let anyone put you in a box!

Our books may be purchased in bulk for promotional, educational or business use. Please contact your local bookseller or IPG Books at orders@ipgbook.com

Library of Congress Control Number: 2018944539
ISBN (hardcover) 978-0-9976085-6-4
ISBN (picture book) 978-0-9976085-7-1

The art in this book was drawn with pencil and colored digitally.
Book design by Emily Love O'Malley

CARDINAL RULE PRESS
5449 Sylvia
Dearborn Heights, MI 48125
Visit us at www.CardinalRulePress.com

BEFORE READING:

* In this story, Travis is picked on because of what he likes to do for fun and what he likes to wear. Ask your child, "Have you ever been picked on for liking something different?"

* Point out the title of the book. Ask your child to pick a word that they think is suiting for their personality (i.e., Creative Ella, Magnificent Anthony)

DURING READING:

* When kids are treating Travis poorly, he does not react with anger. Instead he composes himself before responding. What additional ways can your child think of to react to a bully?

* Discuss what bravery is and how sometimes it can mean being yourself even if other people think it's weird or strange.

AFTER READING:

* Travis is very proud of who he is despite his differences. How are you different and what makes you special?

* Ask your child, "What do you think it would be like if we were all the same?"

For Seth, and for all my theater students past, present, and future.
HC

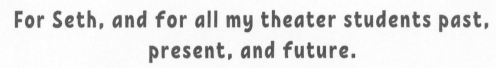

To my parents, who encouraged me to be who I am.
BF

Colorful denim
And glitter galore
Are some of my favorites
To play in, explore.

Dresses and armor:
Pink, black, or green.
I pretend I'm a knight,
A king or a queen.

I tappity-tap.
I rise on my toes.
Whatever the dance,
I'm all set to go.

There are so many things
To like all around.
No limits or range
Holding me down.

Sometimes my classmates,
When on the playground
Like staring and judging
And cutting me down.

"You're a boy!" they exclaim.
"You can't play with a doll.
Just play with your soldiers
Or glove, bat and ball."

"You like to dress up?
You think fairies are cool?"
They bully and hound
With ridiculous rules.

"Boys CAN'T play with that!
It's too girly," they say.
"And girls can't play this!
Better throw it away."

Words tumble toward me
That aren't so kind.
They sting and they poke
Try to enter my mind.

I stand my ground firmly.
Don't let in the hate.
I swish back my hair,
Then set them all straight.

"I am who I am!
There's no boy and girl line.
In sports or in dress-up,
I'll sparkle and shine."

"The toys that we play with,
Or clothes that we wear,
express who we are
And our natural flair."

"A boy can like pink
And a girl can like blue.
It's not weird or strange
To express the true you."

"So judge if you want.
I'll do things my way.
For Dazzling Travis
Has come here to stay!"

JUST LIKE TRAVIS, THESE PEOPLE STRUGGLED AGAINST THE OPINIONS OF OTHERS, BUT THEY PERSEVERED AND SOON DAZZLED IN THEIR OWN WAYS.

Elizabeth Stride was the first American woman to sign a baseball contract. Previously, baseball had been played mostly by men. However, in the 1860s girls began to move from the sidelines onto the fields. Despite some people thinking the sport was only for boys, Lizzie rose above the naysayers and made a career of the game she loved.

Fernando Bujones was a Cuban ballet dancer born in America. As a boy, he was often far outnumbered by the girls in his classes. However, Fernando knew that dancing was where he belonged, and he continued to practice. As a result of all his hard work, he eventually joined the American Ballet Theatre and rose to principal dancer.

Coco Chanel was known for what some people called her "strange" style. Being one of the first people to design suits and trousers for women, she introduced looks that were utterly different than what anyone had seen. Despite some negative opinions, Coco rose above the hate and became one of fashion's most innovative and successful designers.

Langston Hughes was a poet, novelist, playwright, and columnist. In his earlier works, he often wrote about his loneliness as a kid. Though making friends was hard when he was young, Langston continued to dazzle and do what he loved-write! As an adult, he found great success with his writing and became a leader in the Harlem Renaissance.

This story was inspired by one of my former students Seth. Since a young age and into his early teens, Seth always felt different or was told he couldn't do something. However, Seth found theatre and his voice. "I was able to be all the things I dreamed in my head and I found the courage and strength to be me," Seth says. His message to anyone who has ever felt different is, "Don't let people define who you are, be strong and creative, for you will change the world!!"

HANNAH CARMONA is a writer who currently resides in Tennessee. *Dazzling Travis* is her second book and was inspired by her work in children's theater. In addition to being a writer, Hannah is also a mother of two wonderful girls, co-founder of Collective Art School of Tennessee, YouTuber, and actress. When she is not working on her books, Hannah enjoys binge-watching shows on Netflix, avoiding housework, and spending time with her two cats, dog, and iguana.

BRENDA FIGUEROA is a freelance illustrator based in Madrid. She was born in El Salvador, a colorful land of volcanoes, coffee plantations and beautiful sand seashores. At an early age, she developed a deep interest and sensitivity for illustrated books. Her professional background includes a Bachelor's degree in Graphic Design and a Children's Book Illustration MA. She has several years of experience in advertising and a wide range of illustration projects, including published picture books. To learn more, visit: www.brendafigueroa.com